Key Facts

Dragon Lord

To be a Dragon Lord, you must have magic. Every Dragon Lord can control a dragon.

When a dragon is Lord-less, it means their Dragon Lord is gone. They become wild and dangerous.

Lord-less

Tracking

Seb is good at tracking. This means he might find the dragon quicker.

Story Background

Seb really wants to be a Dragon Lord. When he hears about a Lord-less dragon on the loose, he knows he has to find her. This could be his chance to be a Dragon Lord!

BY **KRIS KNIGHT**

ILLUSTRATED BY **ALAN BROWN**

Walkthrough

Read this first - or turn the page to go straight to the story!

The Characters

Seb

Seb wants to be a Dragon Lord but he doesn't have any magic. This doesn't mean he will give up!

The Dragon

The dragon is Lord-less and alone in the mountains. She is wary of others.

The Hunters

The hunters are looking for the dragon. They want to slay her - can Seb get to her first?

The dragon leapt up and Seb let go.

Fire filled the air.
The dragon ran away.

Seb decided to help the dragon.

He got food for both of them.

They escaped together.

Seb did not have magic but he had made friends with a dragon!

THE END.

Level Up...

Answer the questions below. Each correct answer gains you points. Are you a Trainee or a Grand Master?

1 *Multiple Choice:*
Where does Seb hear about the dragon? **1pt**
a) At Dragon School
b) On the road
c) At the inn

2 *Multiple Choice:*
How does Seb find the dragon?
a) He tracks her **1pt**
b) He lays a trap for her
c) He calls her name

3 Why can't the dragon fly away? **2pts**

4 *Fill in the sentence:*
Seb tried to _____ the dragon's wing. **3pts**
Soon they were friends.

5 What is happening in the image below? **2pts**

6 *Multiple Choice:*
Who saves Seb from the hunters in the end? **1pt**
a) A Dragon Lord
b) The innkeeper
c) The dragon

Answers on the next page. Every correct answer earns points (pts) Which level are you?

Level:
0 - 1pts = Trainee
2 - 4pts = Novice
5 - 7pts = Adept
8 - 9pts = Expert
10pts = Grand Master

Explore...

Think about the following:

- Why do you think the dragon let Seb help her? How do you think she felt?

- Do you think Seb will ever become a Dragon Lord? How?

- Where do you think Seb and the dragon will go? What will they do together?

Other Titles